A Horse's Tale
A Colonial Williamsburg Adventure

~ by Susan Lubner illustrated by Margie Moore ~

Abrams Books for Young Readers, New York
in association with The Colonial Williamsburg Foundation

A Note on the Artwork

When visiting Colonial Williamsburg in the early stages of work on *A Horse's Tale*, Margie Moore was greatly impressed by the talent of the tradespeople there. Their generous help with details for the book gave much energy to the project. She found Lancer, the runaway horse in this book, a most heartening character to draw. Her medium for this book is black pen and watercolors on cold press paper.

Library of Congress Cataloging-in-Publication Data:
Lubner, Susan.
A horse's tale / by Susan Lubner ; illustrated by Margie Moore.
p. cm.
Summary: In Williamsburg, Virginia, in colonial days, Lancer the horse runs loose and behaves oddly while his owner and owner's friends try everything they can think of to help him feel better, until Margaret the Milliner realizes that Lancer needs a friend, too.
ISBN-13: 978-0-8109-9490-4 (hardcover)
ISBN-10: 0-8109-9490-9 (hardcover)
[1. Friendship—Fiction. 2. Horses—Fiction. 3. Animals—Fiction. 4. Williamsburg (Va.)—History—Colonial period, ca. 1600–1775—Fiction. 5. Stories in rhyme.] I. Moore, Margie, ill. II. Title.
PZ8.3.L955Hor 2008
[E]—dc22
2007022467

Text copyright © 2008 Susan Lubner and The Colonial Williamsburg Foundation
Illustrations copyright © 2008 The Colonial Williamsburg Foundation

Colonial Williamsburg is a registered trade name of The Colonial Williamsburg Foundation, a not-for-profit educational institution.

Book design by Vivian Cheng

Published in 2008 by Abrams Books for Young Readers,
an imprint of Harry N. Abrams, Inc. All rights reserved.
No portion of this book may be reproduced, stored in a retrieval system, or transmitted in any form or by any means, mechanical, electronic, photocopying, recording, or otherwise, without written permission from the publisher.

Printed and bound in China
10 9 8 7 6 5 4 3 2 1

HNA ▮▮▮▮▮
harry n. abrams, inc.
a subsidiary of La Martinière Groupe
115 West 18th Street
New York, NY 10011
www.hnabooks.com

Colonial Williamsburg
The Colonial Williamsburg Foundation
P.O. Box 1776
Williamsburg, Virginia 23187-1776
www.colonialwilliamsburg.org

To David, my husband and best friend
And to all my wonderful friends
—SL

For my mother, Lillian Kelly
—MM

Margaret the Milliner owned a shop with lots of things to sell:
Hats and bows and velvet cloaks, and other goods as well.

In Williamsburg, Virginia,
While Margaret sat and sewed,
She was startled by the sound of hooves
Pounding up the road.

On this fair day in Williamsburg, something was awry.
Garrick the Gardener's horse ran loose, and Margaret wondered why.

Lancer galloped past the Courthouse. He passed the Magazine.
Turning at Bruton Parish Church, he crossed the Palace Green.

The Town Crier stepped into the street. He began to yell:

"*Hear ye! Hear ye!*" he called out. He rang his shiny bell.

"*A horse is loose!*
A horse is loose!" the Crier did repeat.

He shouted out, "*He's on his way down*
Duke of Gloucester Street!"

Peering through her window, Margaret craned her neck to see.
She watched her good friend Garrick chase his horse, which still ran free.
As Garrick sprinted by her store, he shouted with great force,
"I have the flowers for your shop, but I need to catch my horse!"

Ben the Blacksmith rushed to help. Margaret dashed outside her shop.
They joined the chase to help their friend and coaxed the horse to stop.
Margaret pointed out to Garrick, "Lancer looks so sad."
"Maybe he's ill," suggested Ben, "or maybe he's gone mad."

"Hear ye, hear ye," the Crier sang.

The horse let out a snort.

"Garrick's horse is acting odd, I'm sorry to report!"

"Lancer's troubled." Garrick sighed. "He's acting very strange.
He won't work or pull the cart—aye, that has got to change!
I must deliver all my fruits and vegetables and flowers.
Without my horse to pull the cart, it will take me several hours."

"I'll check his shoes," offered Ben, "to see if they are right.
Horses can feel grumpy if their shoes are on too tight."
Ben led them to his blacksmith shop. The forge was flaming hot.
There were newly forged hooks and nails, a kitchen pan and pot.

Ben removed Lancer's shoes. He wiped off all the dirt.

He double-checked each cleaned-off hoof to make sure nothing hurt.

"His feet look fine," Ben declared. He gave each foot a tap.

"He might be tired," Margaret said. "He probably needs a nap."

"Hear ye, hear ye," sang the Crier.

"Here's the latest news!
Whatever bothers
Garrick's horse, 'tis not
his old horseshoes!"

Ben's horse, Mary, was in the shop and waiting to be shod.

Garrick's horse laid eyes on her. He gave a pleasant nod.

When Garrick tried to leave the shop, Lancer would not budge.

"Indeed, your horse," said Margaret, "still holds some sort of grudge."

Garrick's horse was in the dumps, of that there was no doubt!

But Garrick's friends in Williamsburg were eager to help out.

They pledged to help the best they could. They each would do their part.

For Garrick, too, was feeling down without his horse and cart.

The Grocer brought a bowl of oats, and as a special treat,
He mixed the oats with sugar lumps to make it extrasweet.

The Apothecary came at once.
He stirred a special brew.
"SLURP!" Lancer licked his chops,
But still his mood seemed blue.

The Music Teacher tried to help.
She sang the horse a song.
She thought the tune would perk him up,
But sadly she was wrong.

Sixteen Tailors in the town each measured out some wool.

They stuffed a bag with all the cloth until the bag was full.

They took the scraps to Margaret's shop and handed her the sack.

Margaret sewed a counterpane for that troubled horse's back.

But neither sugar-coated meal, nor set of iron shoes,

Nor magical elixir would shake him from his blues.

Not any form of pampering or singing would improve

Poor Lancer's melancholy mood. He still refused to move.

"**Hear ye, hear ye,**" the Crier of Williamsburg wailed.

"*All attempts to cheer the horse have ultimately failed!*"

Garrick sighed and rubbed his chin. Lancer stood his ground.
Then Garrick motioned everyone to come and gather 'round.
"We may have failed to cheer my horse or move him from his spot,
But I'm thankful for your help! Aye, *friendship* means a lot."

Then something changed that moment. It was something Garrick said!
Lancer nuzzled Mary, then he stomped and shook his head.
Margaret saw his eyes were bright. The horse was on the mend!
Just like all of us, she guessed, the horse must need a friend.

Margaret told the others, "Here's the problem with that horse—
Lancer's feeling lonely, and he wants a friend, of course!"
Ben was quick to offer that his own mare be the one.
"They'll do the chores together—that way work will be more fun!"

From Jamestown Road to Waller Street, with Garrick as their guide,
Garrick's horse went back to work with Mary by his side.
They delivered to the taverns, to every Grocer's door,
And flowers to their favorite place—Margaret the Milliner's store!

"Hear ye, hear ye,"
cheered the Crier.

"The horse has found a friend!
All is well in Williamsburg!
This tale now has an end!"

GLOSSARY

APOTHECARY The apothecary was a type of doctor. He made medicines from chemicals as well as plant materials, such as bark, roots, and flowers. He also sold other items, such as soap, candles, and spices.

BLACKSMITH The blacksmith had a very important job in Williamsburg. He heated iron in a forge, or a coal fire, to make necessary tools and objects for the colonists. Other tradespeople, including the wheelwright, cooper, and saddler, depended on the blacksmith for their tools. Blacksmiths not only made iron horseshoes, but they also shod horses and oxen.

BRUTON PARISH CHURCH The state church in colonial Virginia was the Church of England. Williamsburg was in Bruton Parish. People from all classes gathered in Bruton Parish Church for Sunday services.

COLONIAL A person who lives in a place that is under the rule of a distant country.

COUNTERPANE A blanket or quilt.

COURTHOUSE County courthouses in colonial Virginia served many of the same purposes as courthouses today. People recorded legal documents, such as deeds and wills, and brought civil suits to be decided. People who broke minor laws came to trial in county courthouses.

DUKE OF GLOUCESTER STREET The busy main street in Williamsburg lined with shops, taverns, and homes.

FORGE A coal-burning fireplace in the blacksmith's shop used for heating iron. The forge was made of bricks.

FORGED When iron has been softened and hammered into a new shape, such as a horseshoe or pot, it has been forged.

GROCER In his store, the grocer sold meat, flour, sugar, jams, beverages, and more.

MAGAZINE A building used to store guns and ammunition owned by the Virginia colony and under the control of the governor.

MILLINER A tradesperson or sometimes a shop owner who specialized in making accessories and selling items including cloaks, hats, gloves, shoes, buttons, dresses, and mantles. Many of the items found in the milliner's shop were imported from Europe.

PALACE GREEN The long, tree-lined lawn bounded by a semicircular street and leading up to the Governor's Palace.

SHOD When a blacksmith puts horseshoes on a horse's feet, that horse is being shod.

TAILOR A person (almost always a man in colonial Williamsburg) who makes clothes. Tailors first measure their customers to be sure the clothes they have been hired to make fit properly and are the right size.

TAVERN A restaurant and hotel of the eighteenth century. Tavern keepers served food to local residents and travelers. Sometimes balls and parties were held there. Travelers who visited Williamsburg could get a meal and rent a room in a tavern.

TOWN CRIER The town crier reported the news of the day. His job was to walk through the streets of the town and ring his bell to get people's attention. Then he shouted out the important news.

WILLIAMSBURG, VIRGINIA Williamsburg was the capital of Virginia from 1699 until 1780. Named after William III, the king of England, Williamsburg was an important center of government, politics, and trade. Today, Williamsburg has been carefully restored, with many of its original buildings still standing. Williamsburg welcomes guests to experience what it was like to live during colonial and revolutionary times.